the Toad Prince

Linda Jennings

Based on an idea by Isia Ossuchowska

Illustrated by Georgien Overwater

Macdonald Young Books

Chapter One

Annie lived with the Grindles in a big, grand house in a big, grand street. The Grindles were very, very rich, but Annie wasn't. She worked for the Grindles as their servant.

Although they were very rich, the Grindles were horribly mean.

They paid poor Annie next to nothing, and made her scrub and sweep and cook and darn from dawn to dusk.

She never had a day off, not even at Christmas.

There were three members of the Grindle family – Pa Grindle, Ma Grindle, and Norbert Grindle, their son.

Pa spent all of his time thinking of more and more ways of making loads of money.

Ma Grindle was always very busy checking up on Annie, and ordering her to do this and that.

And when Annie had done it, Ma Grindle would tell her that she hadn't done it properly.

Norbert Grindle had a funny sense of humour. He liked jumping out at Annie from dark corners, or putting spiders down her neck.

You can see why Annie was so dreadfully unhappy working for them.

"I wish I had just one friend," she sighed. "Or a pet – a pet would be lovely."

But of course the Grindles had no pets. Pets cost too much money, for one thing, and for another, no pet would hang around when Norbert was there. Norbert liked pulling wings off flies and tying cans to cats' tails.

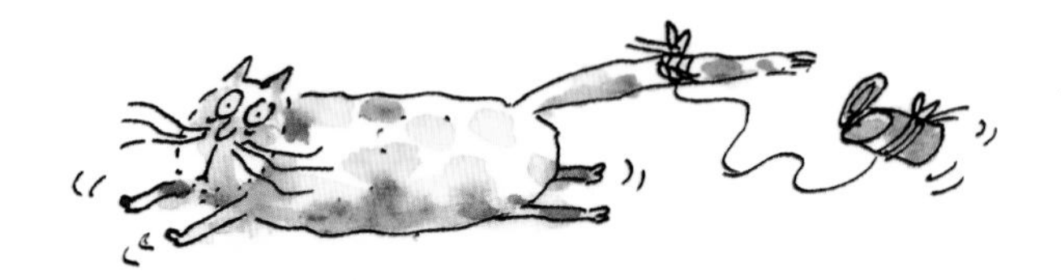

Chapter Two

One day, Annie was out in the stable yard, when she noticed something moving behind a stone. Two round, yellow eyes peered out at her.

"Oh," said Annie. She dropped the Persian rug she had been beating, and took a closer look.

It was a toad. A big, nobbly toad, with a circle of little warts on its head. It looked at her in a friendly way, and blinked. It was a very handsome toad, as toads go, and Annie fell in love with it at once.

"A pet!" she breathed. "A pet of my very own."

She knew at once, of course, that the Grindles wouldn't allow her to have a toad for a pet. But she could keep it hidden in her attic room.

She folded the rug over one arm, and picked up the toad gently.

"You will come to live with me, won't you?" she said.

"Quark!" said the toad, and blinked again.

Annie managed to smuggle the toad up to her attic while Ma Grindle was running her finger over all the furniture in the dining room, to see if Annie had dusted it properly.

There was an old wooden box in the corner, which Annie had brought with her when she came. It held all she owned in the whole world – a couple of books, a raggedy cloak, a gold candlestick her mother had left her when she died, and the woolly blanket Annie had had when she was a baby.

She took everything out of the box, but she put the woolly blanket back again. It would make a nice bed for the toad.

The box had a loose board, and Annie pulled it out to make a gap, so that her toad could breathe properly when the lid was closed.

The toad settled down in his box, and Annie at last went to bed, tired out.

Chapter Three

The next morning, Annie was up and dressed by the cold light of dawn.

"Goodbye, Toad," she whispered to her pet. "I'll sneak some flies and things in to you later on. You must be very hungry." Then she hurried downstairs to clean out the fireplaces.

Annie didn't know that Norbert sometimes sneaked into her room when she was working. He always hoped that she may have hidden away a penny or two from her meagre wages, but he never found anything. Annie spent what money she had on bread and fruit, because the food the Grindles gave her was not enough for a mouse, let alone a growing girl.

Before Annie was half-way through her work, Norbert had tiptoed into her room and found the toad.

With a gleeful giggle, Norbert picked the poor thing up by one of his back legs, and ran downstairs.

Both his parents were sitting at breakfast, reading their papers.

"Hey, Ma! Hey, Pa! Look what I found in Annie's room."

Ma Grindle looked up and shuddered.

"Ugh! How disgusting," she said.

"Get rid of it at once. Throw it on the fire, drown it, I don't care what you do, but TAKE IT AWAY!"

For Norbert had put the toad on his mother's breakfast plate, where it sat peacefully, its eyes blinking and its throat throbbing.

"Hang on a minute," Pa Grindle suddenly said. He put down his newspaper, and stabbed at it with a large, podgy finger. "Read this!" he ordered.

PRINCE CONSTANTINE DISAPPEARS said the headline.

"Oh my goodness," said Ma Grindle. "Has he been kidnapped?"

Norbert was staring at the toad, who stared back at him.

"Are you thinking what I'm thinking, Pa?" he said. "Those little warts on its head, like a crown . . ."

"You're right!" yelled Pa Grindle, springing to his feet and overturning his chair. "Someone's gone and turned the prince into a toad."

Ma Grindle put her chin on her hands.

"Just think," she said. "If we treat this toad right, and manage to turn him back into a prince—"

"We'll get a reward!" cried Norbert.

"Lots and lots of lovely money!" said Pa Grindle, rubbing his hands. He looked sternly at Norbert. "You heard what your mother said – 'if you treat him right'. That doesn't mean holding him up by one leg. You'd better apologize before he tells the king."

Norbert looked sulky. "I can't apologize to a toad—"

"DO IT!"

And Norbert did.

"The Toad Prince wants some breakfast," said Ma Grindle. "Tell Annie to bring him a plate of the best smoked salmon."

"But that was for my supper—" began Pa Grindle.

"Think of the reward!"

"All right, all right," grumbled Pa, and sent for Annie at once.

Chapter Four

Annie went pale when she saw her pet sitting on the breakfast plate. Horrible Norbert had taken him from her room, she knew that at once. But now did they plan to eat him?

"This," said Pa Grindle, "is Prince Constantine, unfortunately magicked into a Toad Prince. He is to be treated like royalty, which, of course, he is.

Only the very best food. And you will prepare the Crimson Bedroom for him to sleep in."

"It's a bit big for a toad," began Annie nervously. "He'd feel lost in it."

"Don't you *dare* argue with me, Miss," roared Pa Grindle. "Just do as you're told."

“It’s my toad,” whispered Annie, but not so that anyone could hear her.

All that day Annie was rushed off her feet. Ma Grindle inspected the Royal Suite as she called it, and she made Annie scrub the floor and polish the furniture three times before she was satisfied that it was good enough for the Toad Prince to sleep in.

Annie suggested that she could find the toad a jarful of flies from the garden, but Ma Grindle shrieked at her:

"Flies! D'you expect Prince Constantine to eat flies!"

She waggled her finger at Annie, and glared into her frightened eyes.

"If you *dare* do anything to offend the prince, then I'll see to it that you work all night as well as all day. If you *dare* to rob us of our reward . . ."

Annie wondered what the Grindles would do to her if she did.

Annie was not allowed to put her Toad Prince into his grand new bedroom. Ma Grindle insisted on doing this herself.

Annie crept up to her attic that night, tired out as usual, and stared unhappily at the toad's empty box with the blanket in it.

"He'll be so lonely," she thought.

Chapter Five

The next day, Annie brought in a plateful of smoked salmon and scrambled egg for the Toad Prince's breakfast. He was sitting on a velvet chair, but he didn't seem very hungry.

"Now," said Pa Grindle, barely glancing at Annie, "it's a well-known fact that toads can be changed back into princes by a single kiss."

"I don't mind kissing him, Pa," interrupted Norbert, "even though kissing a toad is pretty yucky."

"Silence!" roared his father. "How dare you insult the prince. And of course you can't kiss him. It has to be a girl—" He looked at his wife, doubtfully. "I suppose you could try." Ma Grindle giggled and fluttered her eyelashes. She got up from the table and crouched down beside the toad.

"Nice Prince," she murmured, looking rather silly, and gave him a peck on his warty head.

"On his mouth, Ma!" cried Norbert.

But when Ma Grindle kissed the Toad Prince on his mouth, he still sat there, looking every inch a toad.

"What shall we do?" cried Ma. "There's no use in keeping him if he doesn't change back into a prince again.

We won't get any reward for sending a toad back to the king."

"I'll try if you like," Annie suddenly broke in timidly. "I'm a girl."

"You're a servant," snarled Pa Grindle. "And don't forget it!" He pushed her out of the room and slammed the door behind her.

Later that day, Annie saw Norbert staggering out of the front door with a big notice under his arm. She could just see what it said:

At first everyone seemed very excited to see the Toad Prince, but then they began to mutter among themselves.

"He doesn't do anything," someone said, "he just sits there."

"He looks just like an ordinary toad to me."

"I kissed him, and nothing happened."

"It's just those Grindles trying to make money out of us."

As everyone got angrier and angrier, the Grindles pushed them all out again and locked the gates. They had made quite a pile of money.

Chapter Six

Annie was in the kitchen the next day, washing up, when Norbert came bursting in, shrieking with laughter.

"Guess what!" he shouted at her. "Prince Constantine has returned! He didn't have a spell put on him. Your toad isn't a prince at all! Serve the parents right for being so stupid. Ha, ha, ha."

Annie felt a shiver of fear. "What will you do to my toad?"

"I'm just wondering whether I'll skin him alive, or burn him, or pull his legs off," laughed Norbert. "Ma and Pa are pretty mad. They're particularly mad with you, for bringing the toad here in the first place!"

Annie gave a little cry. She sprang away from the sink, and pushed past Norbert.

She dashed from the kitchen, slamming the door behind her, ran down the corridor into the hall, and up the stairs. She reached the Crimson Bedroom just as Norbert arrived at the foot of the stairs.

The toad was sitting on the table by the four-poster bed, happily staring into space. He had no idea of the dreadful fate that Norbert planned for him.

Annie ran across the room, and scooped him up in her hand. She could hear Norbert pounding up the stairs.

"Not a croak from you," she warned.

She dived under the four-poster bed, and lay there for a moment, feeling the toad throbbing in her hands. Then, as Norbert stormed across the room, she slid from under the bed, and ran out of the door, down the staircase and into the kitchen again. Behind her, she could hear Norbert shouting for his parents.

"I'm running away," she gasped. "I can't stand it here any longer."

Annie stumbled out of the door, and ran down the path to the rose garden. Here she stopped for breath. She let the toad sit on her hand in the sunshine, and she looked deep into his eyes.

"Dear Toad," she said. "I'm sorry about all this rush and bother, but your life's in danger—"

Even now she could hear the Grindles opening the kitchen door . . .

"What shall we do, Toad?" cried Annie, looking wildly around.

She knew it was hopeless. The Grindles had locked the gates, and the walls had spikes along the top.

"Oh Toad," said Annie, in tears, "the Grindles will get us after all!"

"Quark!" said the Toad, gazing at her with his big, beautiful yellow eyes. "Kiss me!" he seemed to say . . .

Chapter Seven

The Grindles blundered into the rose garden.

"Ha! We've got her cornered now," cried Pa. "Her and that disgusting toad!"

"Yes!" shrieked Norbert. "There's the toad – look, behind the statue—"

"Two toads," said Ma Grindle. "There are *two* toads!"

"GET THEM!" ordered Pa Grindle.

But it was too late. The toads had crawled out through a gap in the hedge and out of harm's way.

There was no sign of Annie at all.

The Grindles went back to their big grand house, but they did not live happily ever after. Norbert married a rich lady, who nagged at him all day and made him clean his own shoes and darn his own socks.

Pa Grindle went on making loads and loads of money, which he kept in Annie's old attic room. One day the

whole house collapsed with the weight of all that gold, and the Grindles were left homeless. They had to spend everything they had on building a new home. So much good did all that money do them.

But the toad and Annie *did* live happily ever after, by a big pond in the peaceful garden next door.